X-IO SOLAR SYS

JUPITER

SATURN

URANUS

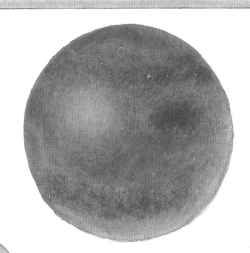

NEPTUNE

OUTER PLANETS

PLUTO

NO. OF MOONS	APPROX. DIAMETER
MERCURY: 0	3,000 MILES
VENUS: 0	7,500 MILES
EARTH: 1	7,900 MILES
MARS: 2	4,200 MILES
CELESTIA: 7	1 MILE
JUPITER: 16	89,000 MILES
SATURN: 18	75,000 MILES
URANUS: 15	32,000 MILES
NEPTUNE: 8	31,000 MILES
PLUTO: 1	1,800 MILES

DAVE AND JANE
IN
OUTER SPACE

BOB KNOX

RIZZOLI
NEW YORK

Dear Reader,

One day last winter, I found a mysterious-looking book, titled **The X-10 Diary,** stuffed inside my mailbox. It seems to have been written by alien children who were visiting our solar system 70 million years ago—when dinosaurs roamed the earth! This entire diary has been reproduced without any changes on the following pages. Whether it's authentic or not, nobody can say. Anyway, I hope you all enjoy it.

Best wishes,

Bob Knox

Connecticut, 1995

Publisher's Note

Even though we think this diary might be a big hoax, we still can't identify the substance on which it is written. It feels like wax, bends like aluminum foil, and smells like chocolate.

Rizzoli, New York

THE X-10 DIARY
WRITTEN BY DAVE AND JANE
PICTURES BY VINCENT
X-10
DAVE JANE
V

ear Diary,

Today is the day! Jane and I will finally take our "Space Test in Advanced Rocketeering" or "S.T.A.R." for short. We have to fly a real spaceship on a real mission in outer space! If we pass our S.T.A.R., then we get our very own spaceship like everyone else here on Zarp. We're a little nervous, but they say that's normal for 10-year olds. Three hours until lift-off!

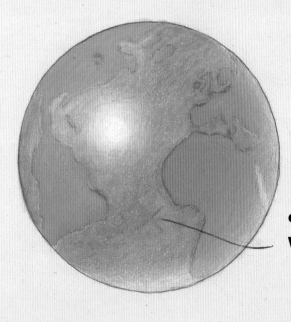

Our beautiful planet Zarp— free from war and disease. We live here.

A view of Zarp and its space stations.

Our official "S.T.A.R." orders are: "Go to the nearby X-10 solar system. Travel through time and space, collecting specimens and data from all ten planets. Go in peace and be prepared to help any and all lifeforms. STAY AWAY FROM PLANET EARTH. Report back to Zarp within 40 days."

MINERVA

Our stellar powered "S.T.A.R." spaceship

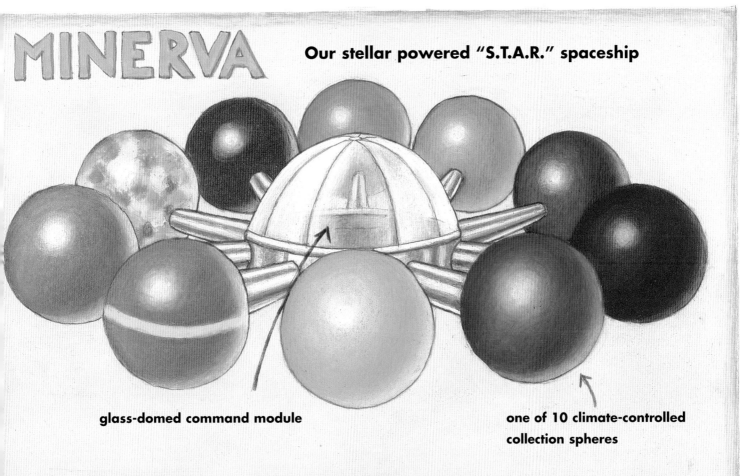

glass-domed command module

one of 10 climate-controlled
collection spheres

Minerva is a huge old clunker, but she can still go from zero to lightspeed in 5 seconds!
The specimens we collect from each X-10 planet will be stored in Minerva's ten spheres
for later study. Docking bays for shuttle craft are under the command module.

OUR SHUTTLES / OUR CREW

2 HOURS,
17 MINUTES
9 SECONDS
'TILL
LIFT-OFF!

"Derby"

"Cowboy"

Vincent, our
android and
the mission
artist

Orbit, our dog
(a satellite Retriever)

(Smart) Alec
(know-it-all) Robot

DAY 1: We're on our way! As we approach X-10 Alec plugs our time machine into Minerva's engines. Turning the knob to "B.N." (Before Now) lets us travel anytime in the past. Turning the knob to "A.N." (After Now) takes us into the

future. We can return to the present by moving the knob to "N" (Now). This means we can now travel anytime/anywhere in X-10!

DAY 2: Alec takes Orbit for a space-walk.

Nearing Mercury, we notice a big hole in its outer shell!

We decide to go inside. Strong winds batter the ship!

We land on the warm inner core (like a nut inside a shell). There are people down here! They seem very happy to see us and give us many gifts, which we

transport to one of the collection spheres. As thanks, we offer them a ride out to view the stars. Odd, they're not at all upset about the sky hole!

We return to Mercury after a short ride, Wow! The hole has already healed itself and we cannot re-enter! Our guests must now stay with us. Oh no, the darn time-machine knob won't turn left anymore. Now we can only travel in the present or future direction.

DAY 3: We approach Venus, where we perform a complicated space-writing procedure for our Space Test.

We break through the Venus clouds to find a tropical paradise! We carefully collect exotic plants. There are people here, too! They are peaceful and shy. We hand out official "S.T.A.R." hats as gifts.

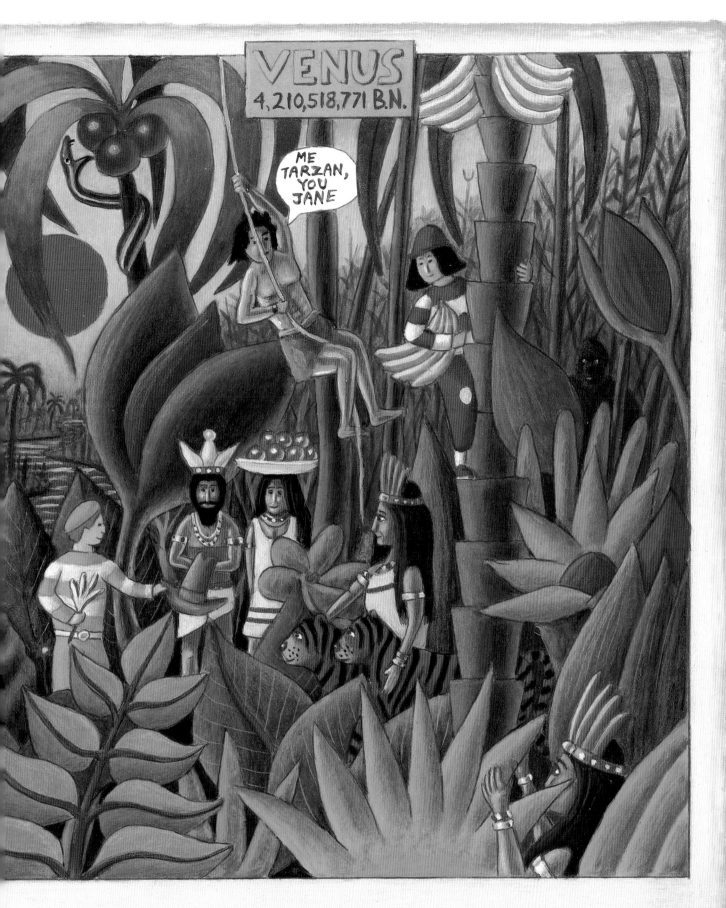

When night approaches, they speak fearfully of a big gorilla, but we don't see any such ape. They beg to spend a night up in the safety of Minerva. We say, "O.K., friends, but one night only."

We take our guests to the movies—X-10 has it all!

We fly to Mars, avoiding Earth as ordered.

DAY 4: A Venus typhoon prevents our landing. We must return our guests later.

DAY 5: We launch satellites (a S.T.A.R. requirement) from Deimos, one of two Martian moons. Tomorrow, we explore the Red Planet!

DAY 6: There's life on Mars! The silly little green Martians are too busy throwing tomatoes to even notice us! We collect valuable red specimens for further study.

DAY 7: As we leave Mars, Dave makes milkshakes for all our guests. They're out of this world! We set a course for planet Celestia.

DAY 8: We play hide and seek among strange Celestia moons. The planet's sky is so colorful, we decide to take a closer look tomorrow!

DAY 9: Nobody here—only an abandoned amusement park! Dave tries out "The Strong Man." Weird cracking everywhere. Suddenly, Alec arrives and shouts, "Leave here at once! Hurry!"

CELESTIA composition: plaster, plastic, polyester Planet surface has been constantly pounded. Will break apart soon! DANGER! STAY AWAY!!

We zoom away just as Celestia crumbles to bits! A close call! Why did this happen?

The answer is on this page we overlooked in our X-10 guide.

DAY 10: We hitch a ride on a comet for the 5 million mile ride to Jupiter. We get S.T.A.R. bonus points for this maneuver!

Watching "fireworks" on Io, the volcanic moon of Jupiter. Tomorrow, we'll record weather data near the Great Red Spot.

THE SUN WE'RE NOW HALFWAY FINISHED WITH OUR MISSION JUPITER MERCURY VENUS EARTH MARS ASTEROID BELT

DAY 11: Just outside the Red Spot, we notice odd signals from a floating island. A zillionaire greets us. He says he traded his spaceship for this island of luxury a long time ago. Turns out he is our long-lost great uncle Ebenezer!

SATURN URANUS NEPTUNE PLUTO

Despite all his riches, Eb is lonely and misses life back on Zarp. We tell him, "You can come with us—we'll be home in 2 weeks!" Eb exclaims, "Hurray! Zarp, here I come!"

DAY 12-14: It's a very long flight to Saturn. Eb wins 131 Moonopoly games!

DAY 15: Saturn at dawn. Alec and Vincent test the upper atmosphere under the arching rings. Minerva's sensors detect a faint heartbeat from the inner Saturn ring. LIFE! We'll investigate at once!

Amazing discovery! The inner ring is composed of billions of unidentifiable eggs! We carefully gather some for later study at the famed Zarp Egg Institute.

THE SUN HERE IS 350 TIMES WEAKER THAN ON EARTH →

OPEN 42 YEARS A NIGHT!

HELIUM

← ANYONE FOR POOL?

E-GLUE SERVICE STATION

DAY 16-17: Journey to Titania, a Uranus moon. We detach the spheres and fly solo (another "S.T.A.R." requirement).

7-UP

ROOT BEER

DAVE, JANE, AND ORBIT

DAY 18: Our X-10 guide lists a nearby service station on Uranus. We go there to service the ship and shuttles. There are people inside! They are very jovial! They call themselves S-ski-mos and live in snow houses called E-Glues.

They are in the middle of 42-year-long Uranus night and they're very bored and restless. We invite them to ride with us for a while, move into one of our spheres, and meet our other X-10 guests. Overjoyed, they accept our offer.

S-ski-mos play happily in the brightly lit Uranus sphere. Temperature is set comfortably at minus 50°c.

A U.F.O. near Neptune!

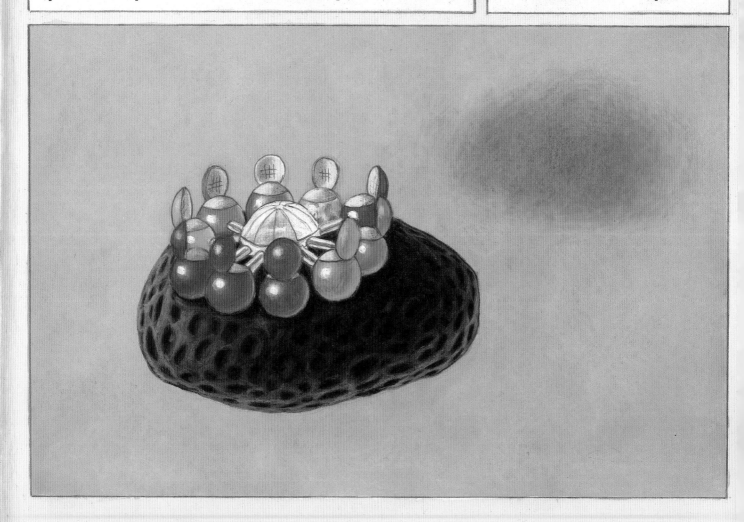

DAY 19: We re-charge Minerva's stellar-power cells on Naiad, Neptune's inner-most moon (a S.T.A.R. requirement). Neptune is so close, it fills the entire sky!

DAY 20: X-10 guide says Neptune has great fishing, so Alec activates our watertight shield and takes the ship down 500 feet. We gather various fish for the Zarp Planetary Aquarium. (more S.T.A.R. bonus points!)

Fish are all collected when disaster strikes! We get caught in a giant Neptune whirlpool!

After spinning down for hours, we suddenly come out clear on the other side of the planet!

DAY 21: A little dizzy, we make our way out toward Pluto.

DAY 22: We glide silently over Charon, one of Pluto's moons. This dark, lonely outpost of X-10 is a little scary. Luckily, Pluto is the last stop on our mission.

DAY 23: Floating over Pluto, we employ ultra-violet, infrared flashlights to scan the planet (another S.T.A.R. requirement). We see weird figures that fade quickly in the light. Impossible to make contact. We collect only memories and dreams.

DAY 24: Our X-10 mission is now complete! Hurray! On the way home, we park briefly on Earth's moon to celebrate our success with a huge party!

Suddenly—RED ALERT! A very severe meteor shower is approaching! We rush to the control room!

Emergency lift-off! Hurry! Meteors are closing in on us!

A frantic get-away! Oh no! We're hit! We're pulled into Earth's atmosphere! Prepare to crash land! Mayday! Mayday!

Losing altitude! Ship out of control! Horrible dinosaurs all around us! Exploding meteors! Brace for impact!

Everything goes black. We come to hours later. Everything is eerily still. Can't see a thing outside—too much smoke. Terrified, we wait.

DAY 29: Five days later, we finally dare to venture out. The dinosaurs are all gone! Amazingly, everyone is O.K., but what a mess! Some spheres are missing, others are cracked and leaking. This violates "S.T.A.R." law #1—Never transplant lifeforms to other planets! We're in BIG trouble! There go all those S.T.A.R. bonus points. **DAY 30:** We start repairs. **DAYS 31-32:** The shuttles and Eb's copter depart to find the missing spheres. How will we ever pass our S.T.A.R. now?

DAY 33: Shuttles locate each missing sphere in a separate climate zone on Earth. Amazing! Our guests not only survive the crash, but insist on remaining where they landed, despite our pleas for them to return to the ship!

Oh boy! We've accidentally populated the Earth with humans! No time left to clean up our "spill." We must fix our ship now and get home before our 40-day deadline or we'll fail our test!

DAYS 34-38: We hurry to finish repairs. Missing spheres are returned to Minerva and re-attached. Our only chance to pass our S.T.A.R. is to keep our accident a secret. We have just two hours until the final lift-off for home.

DAY 40: Zarp spaceport in sight! The official "S.T.A.R." committee is waiting to award us with our very own ship! Looks like we passed our test! Hurray!

P.S. One year later we're here on future Earth to hide this diary from the S.T.A.R. Committee so they'll never find out about our accident. Wow! Things have really changed here! We're also leaving our diary as a gift to all Earthlings who wonder about their true origins. What can we say? Accidents happen!

Love your beautiful planet!

Dave and Jane

First published in the United States of America in 1995 by
Rizzoli International Publications, Inc.
300 Park Avenue South, New York, New York 10010

Library of Congress Cataloging-in-Publications Data

Knox, Bob.
    Dave and Jane in outer space / by Bob Knox.
        p.   cm.
    Summary: The diary of two ten-year-olds on an
intergalactic trip seventy million years ago.
    ISBN 0-8478-1916-7 (hc)
    [1. Interplanetary voyages—Fiction.   2. Diaries—
Fiction.]
I. Title.
PZ7.K77Dah   1995
[Fic]—dc20   95-13346
                                             CIP
                                             AC

Designed by Barbara Balch

Printed and bound in Singapore

THE OFFICIAL
X-10
GUIDEBOOK

IMPORTANT INFO. ABOUT ALL 10 PLANETS AND 68 X-10 MOONS. INCLUDES STAR MAPS, TIME-SPACE DIMENSIONS, AND MORE!

RIZZOLI X-10

VENUS FLY-IN
ADMIT ONE
50¢ AN X-10 THEATRE

PHOTOS OF DAVE AND JANE'S FRIENDS

THIS BOOK IS DEDICATED TO JULIAN AND NELLIE
— B.K. 1995

make right turn after sun, go straight 5 million miles. pass little Dipper. – 1st planet on R. (look out for black holes)

"THREE BROTHERS" ROCKET REPAIR
THE "E-GLUE"
NORTH POLE, URANUS
(900) 000-0000
ASK FOR NIK, HANNES, OR PHIL

SPACE STATION 1¢

BUBBLE HOMES 4¢

MERCURY CAMEL'S HAIR ↑

"MARTIAN" BUBBLE GUM
MARS CANDY CO.

EXPIRES 1-5-1031
75¢ OFF!
ZARP-L-RATION DOG FOOD 99 OZ. SIZE

BEWARE OF METEORS!
FROM CELESTIA FORTUNE-TELLER BOOTH

A VENUS ↑ 4-LEAF CLOVER